Власть Тьмы

The Power of Darkness

By Leo Nikolayevich Tolstoy

Adapted to one act by Don Bliss

"Everybody thinks of changing humanity, but nobody thinks of changing themselves."
-- Tolstoy

Freetown, Massachusetts
"Putting local pen to global paper"
www.sugarhousepress.com

"The Power of Darkness: One Act Adaptation"
Printed in U.S.A.
ISBN 978-0-557-51372-7

Important Note

All producers of "The Power of Darkness: One Act Adaptation " shall credit Don Bliss as the original author of this work on all programs, posters, webpages and other printed matter such as paid advertising under the producer's control. The credit to the author shall be not less than fifty percent (50%) of the size of type used for the title of the play. Said billing shall appear on a separate line following the title of the play and shall appear in the following form:

"(Name of Producer)
presents
The Power of Darkness: One Act Adaptation
by Don Bliss

original stage production by the Viking Theater Company"

The Power of Darkness: One Act Adaptation was originally performed on Saturday, March 3, 2001 with the following actors: Erik Bartlett, *Pyotr*; Krystle Flanders, *Anisya*; Becca Lavalley, *Akulina*; Becky Yannizze, *Anyutka*; Dereck Quaranto, *Nikita*; Jarrod Barbetta, *Akim*; Jen Roberts, *Matryona*; Erin Potter, *Marina*; Carl Peterson, *Mitrich*; K.C. O'Donnell and Michelle Ferreira as neighbors; Jarrid Lopes as the Matchmaker; Mike Murphy as Akulina's Bridegroom; Andrew McDowell as the Best Man; Mike Gouthro as the Policeman; Kevin Churbuck as the Magistrate; Wedding Ensemble: Danny Tatlow, Jared Gabrey, Rob Murphy, Matt Barthe, Marc Felix, John Medeiros, Clay Corey, Lisa Repetti, Kara Bassett, Natara Andrews, Ashley Taber, Jenn Hickey, Kelly Knight, Melody Franklin, Courtney Smith, Liz Enos, Melynda Booker, Marcus Cooper

Dramatis Personae

Pyotr, a rich peasant, forty-two years old, married for the second time, morbid, ailing
Anisya, his wife, thirty two years old, a dressy woman
Akulina, Pyotr's daughter from his first marriage sixteen years old, hard of hearing, simple-minded
Anyutka, his second daughter, ten years old
Nikita, their hired man; twenty-five years old, a dandy
Akim, Nikita's father, fifty years old, an insignificant, uncomely, God-fearing peasant
Matryona, his wife, fifty years old, evil and scheming
Marina, an orphan girl, twenty-two years old
Mitrich, an old, hired hand, a retired soldier
A **neighbor**
Another **neighbor**
A **matchmaker**, a sullen and greedy peasant
His **wife**
A policeman
The Best Man
Akulina's Bridegroom
The Magistrate
Guests, women, girls, people at the wedding.

Introduction

On the surface, this play is about the spiritual choices we are all faced with in life- the path of righteousness - offered by God (represented in the play by Nikita's father) or the path of wickedness and sin, which is facilitated by our earthly desires (represented by Nikita's mother). Nikita, the central figure must ultimately choose which path to take, but as the Russian proverb goes – *when one claw is caught, the whole bird is lost.* There is a danger, however in applying too narrow an interpretation to this piece.

We live in an age that bears many resemblances to 19th century Russia. Not since 19th Century Russia has a society been as concerned and focused on violence as the one in which we live today. Young people are entering adulthood in a society which simultaneously glorifies and abhors violence. A whole generation has grown up surrounded by cultural and historical markers of senseless violence such as the Oklahoma City bombing, the Columbine High School shooting, September 11th, and countless other incidents and reminders.

A great debate raged in Tolstoy's day as well, about the use of violence to achieve personal and political change. Despite many humanitarian achievements which marked the reign of Tsar Alexander II, the people were still in the grips of powerlessness and disenfranchisement that led to the rise of several revolutionary societies. There were numerous assassination attempts on the Tsar. Finally, in 1881, a plot led by Sophia Perovskaya, (a young woman of noble lineage) horrified the nation. A bomb was thrown under the Tsar's iron-clad carriage, injuring several members of his guard. The bomber was arrested on the spot. Then, despite the coachman's fervent pleas to stay in the carriage – (he insisted he could drive the damaged carriage out of danger), Alexander insisted upon stepping out to see to his wounded guards. He approached the bomber

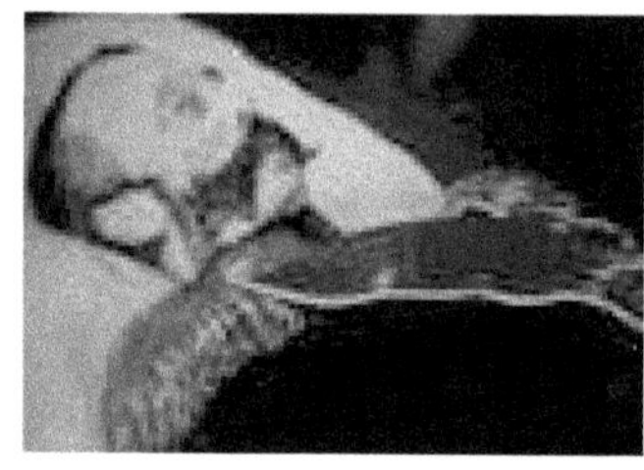

and asked him something; and as he passed close by, another young man threw a bomb that blew the Tsars legs away. Alexander II was dragged on a sled, leaving a trail of his blood on the snow to the Winter Palace, where he died hours later. All of the assassins, including Perovskaya were arrested and convicted within two months. A nationwide debate on the death penalty ensued which is reminiscent of current day political/ethical debates.

Russia's intelligentsia was divided on the usefulness and the ramifications of a public execution. Dosteovsky described the mood of the day: "*The definitions and boundary lines between good and evil have disappeared.... disintegration is everywhere, for everything has come apart, and no bonds remain.*"

Tolstoy's reaction to the horrible assassination of Alexander II was to espouse a utopian and non-violent world in which individuals took responsibility for their actions. *"I now see clearly that my faith"* he said, "*-my only real faith - that which apart from my animal instincts gave impulse to my life - was a belief in perfecting myself.*" Tolstoy's fear was that if the old order were ended by violence, the new order would have to be *maintained* by it. Those who opposed Tolstoy's views branded him as simplistic while they themselves continued to use centuries of oppression as a justification for the use of violence to achieve desired personal and social ends. Tolstoy realized that centuries of oppression and extreme poverty created an excuse for common folk to steal and cheat and kill with impunity. For the state to exercise violent oppression in response to this would guarantee more of the same, in his view. *"The Power of Darkness*" was one of many pieces written to illustrate this.

The value of this piece, then to today's audience is not solely as a proselytizing piece, but as an exhortation to accept personal responsibility not just for our conduct, but for our society as well.

В Тёмном Лесе

(In the Dark Forest)

1. В тёмном лесе, В тёмном лесе,
В тёмном лесе, В тёмном лесе
залесью,залесью.

2. Распашу-ль я, Распашу-ль я,
Распашу-ль я, Распашу-ль я,
пашенку,пашенку.

3. Я посею-ль, Я посею-ль,
Я посею-ль, Я посею-ль,
лён конопель, лён конопель.

4. Уродился, Уродился, Уродился, Уродился,
мой конопель, мой зеленой.

5. Тонок долог, Тонок долог,
Тонок долог, Тонок долог,
бел волокнист, бел волокнист.

6. Как повадился, Как повадился,
Как повадился, Как повадился,
вор воробей,вор воробей.

7. На коноплю, На коноплю,
На коноплю, На коноплю,
летати, летати.

8. Мою конопельку, мою зеленую,
Мою конопельку, мою зеленую,
клевати, клевати.

9. В тёмном лесе, В тёмном лесе,
В тёмном лесе, В тёмном лесе,
залесью, залесью.

10. Распашу-ль я, Распашу-ль я,
Распашу-ль я, Распашу-ль я,
пашенку,пашенку.

11. В тёмном лесе, В тёмном лесе, В тёмном
лесе, В тёмном лесе, залесью, залесью.

F Tyomnom Lesseh

1.Ftyom nom lesseh, Ftyom nom lesseh,
Ftyom nom lesseh, Ftyom nom lesseh, Zalesyu, zalesyu

2.Raspashul ya, Raspashul ya, Raspashul ya, Raspashul ya,
Pashenku, pashenku.

3.Ya poseyul, ya poseyul, Ya poseyul, ya poseyul
Lyon konopell, lyon konopell

4.Urodilsa, urodilsa, Urodilsa, urodilsa
Moy konopell, moy zellenoy

5.Tonok dollug, tonok dollug, Tonok dollug, tonok dollug
Bell voloknist, bell voloknist.

6.Kak povadilsa, kak povadilsa, Kak povadilsa, kak povadilsa
Vor vorabey, vor vorabey

7.Na konoplyu, na konoplyu, Na konoplyu, na konoplyu
Leyta tee, leyta tee

8.Moyu konopelku, moyu zellenuyu, Moyu konopelku,
moyu zellenuyu, Klay va tee, klay va tee.

9.Ftyom nom lesseh, Ftyom nom lesseh,
Ftyom nom lesseh, Ftyom nom lesseh, Zalesyu, zalesyu

10.Raspashul ya, Raspashul ya, Raspashul ya, Raspashul ya,
Pashenku, pashenku.

11.Ftyom nom lesseh, Ftyom nom lesseh,
Ftyom nom lesseh, Ftyom nom lesseh, Zalesyu, zalesyu

SCENE 1

The scene is PYOTR'S *spacious peasant collage.* PYOTR *sits on a bench mending a horse collar.* ANISYA *and* AKULINA *are knitting and singing 'V Tyomnom Lese'.*

PYOTR *(looks out the window).* Again the horses are out. Nikita, hey, Nikita! He's deaf! *(Listens to the women)* That's enough, can't hear a thing.

NIKITA'S VOICE *(from the yard-side of the house).* What?

PYOTR. Bring in the horses.

NIKITA' S VOICE. I'll bring 'em in, gimme time.

PYOTR *(shaking his head).* These hired men! Give you only trouble. Nikita! You go, huh, one of you? Akul, go bring 'em in.

AKULINA. What, the horses?

PYOTR. What else?

AKULINA. Right away. *(Exits)*

PYOTR. He's a slacker, that fellow, waste of money. Turns his back on you, just turns it.

ANISYA. You're right smart-you sit on the bench. Expect others to do it all.

PYOTR. I expect nothing from you at all!

ANISYA. You hand out ten jobs at once and then curse. Sitting on your duff it's easy to give orders.

PYOTR *(sighing).* Chatter-that's all he does. Really, shouldn't keep him.

ANISYA *(mimicking him).* Wouldn't keep him. You yourself get a move on, then you could talk.

AKULINA *(enters).* All I had to do was close the gate, they were already in-

PYOTR. And where's Nikita?
AKULINA. Nikita? Standing in the street.
PYOTR. What's he standing for?
AKULINA. What's he standing for? He's standing round the corner, he's chatting.
PYOTR. You can never get any sense out of her. And who's he chatting with?
AKULINA *(not having heard)*. What?
ANYUTKA *(runs in. To her mother)*. Nikita's mother and father've come after him. Taking him home to stay.
ANISYA. Go on, Anyutka!
ANYUTKA. It's a fact! Cross my heart! *(laughs)* I'm passing by, and Nikita himself says: 'Good-bye, I'm leaving you', he says. And he laughs. (*Exits.*)
ANISYA. (*to* PYOTR) You're glad to let him go-so's you don't have to feed him. And the winter comes and I have to do it all by myself, work like a horse.
PYOTR. You don't know what you're saying, what do you jabber on for?
ANISYA. I ain't going to work for you. Enough, no more. Work yourself.
PYOTR. Yeah, enough. What're you so mad for? You're any-one's piece of meat.
ANISYA. And you're a mad dog! Nobody gets any work out of you, ... and no pleasure neither. You just nag all the time. A big threatening stud-dog, that's you.
PYOTR *(spits and dresses)*. I've got to go find out what's up. *(Exits)*
ANISYA *(after him)*. Stinking devil! big-nosed!
AKULJNA. What're you scolding Pa for?

ANISYA. Go to hell, you fool. Shut up.
AKULINA (goes *up to the door).* I know what you're scolding for. You're an old fool yourself, you're a bitch. I'm not scared of you.
ANISYA. You what? *(Jumps up and looks for something* to *hit her with)* Look out, I'll smash you.
AKULINA *(having opened the door).* You're a bitch, a devil, that's what you are. Devil, bitch, bitch, devil! *(Runs off)*
ANISYA *(alone reflectively).* Come, he says, to my wedding. What's that they've thought up? To marry him? Why? I can't live without him. I won't let him go!
NIKITA *(enters, looks around. Seeing that* ANISYA *is alone, goes quickly up to her. In a whisper).* The old man came, wants to take me away - orders me home. Once and for all, he says, we're going to marry you, and you live at home.
ANISYA. So, get married. What's it to me?
NIKITA. Stop it, Anisya. Really, do I want to forget you? Not on my life. I'll come back to you.
ANISYA. I'd sure need you an awful lot married. It's all your idea. You've been making eyes at that doll of yours, that Marinka, a long time now.
NIKITA. Marinka!? I need her like a--! She's just a slut that sleeps with all the men! If I wanted to go, I'd of gone long ago.
ANISYA. But just remember. If not today then tomorrow the old man'll die. We'll have a church wedding, and you'll be the master. . . *(breaks down)* Will you keep on loving me?
NIKITA *(embraces her).* Like this! You've always been so close to me--

(MATRYONA *enters and for a long time crosses herself in of the icon;* NIKITA *and* ANISYA *move away from each other.)*
MATRYONA. So what I saw I didn't see, what I heard I didn't hear Why not play around? But the master out in the yard's asking for you, son.
NIKITA. I came in for something.
MATRYONA. I know, I know, my dear, for something which, most of the time, the women have for you. Go on, my dear, we'll work it all out for you. (NIKITA. e*xits*)
ANISYA. So how can I, Auntie Matryona, keep it from you. You know everything. I sinned, I fell in love with your son.
MATRYONA. Now, that's something. Ah, dearie, Auntie Matryona's been around, been around, been all over. Auntie Matryona, I tell you, sweetie, can see a yard through the ground. I know everything, sweetie! I know what young wives want to give sleeping powders for. Brought some. *(Unties the knot in her kerchief, takes out a packet of powders)* Auntie Matryona was young, too. I see, sweetie, your old man's worm-eaten, all worm-eaten. Poke him with a pitchfork, no blood'll come out. You'll see, you'll bury him by spring. And is my son not a good man? Am I my own boy's enemy?
ANISYA. Just so he don't leave us.
MATRYONA. And he won't leave, sweetie.
ANISYA. If Nikita goes I won't go on living!
MATRYONA. That's how it is when you're young. I know what you mean! You're a woman full of life, to live with such an old man--

ANISYA. Believe me, Auntie, he's hateful, he's hateful to me, the old long-nosed dog; I can't no more look him in the eye-

MATRYONA. Yeah, that's how it is. Here, look here. *(In a whisper, looking around)* I was at the old man's, see, for some powders. He give me two handfuls of drugs. Look here. This, he says, is a sleeping powder. Give, he says, just one--he'll fall into such a sleep you could walk on him. And this, he says, is such a drug, give it to him, he says, in what he drinks-there's no trace at all, but its power's great. Seven times, he says, a pinch at a time. Just give it the seven times. And the freedom, he says, will come to her soon.

ANISYA. 0-o-o-o. What is it? *(Matryona whispers in her ear)* It also works for cockroaches- *(Suddenly stops talking)* AKIM *enters, crosses himself in front of the icon.)*

PYOTR *(enters and sits down)*. So what d'you think, Uncle Akim?

AKIM. It'd be better, Pyotr Ignatich, be a bit better, now, it'd be better- Somehow it isn't a- The mischief, I mean. I'd like it, now, I'd like the fellow, I mean, to stick to the job. But if you could, now, a-It'd be better so-

PYOTR. And, you know what, Uncle Akim, you know, you can't believe these girls. Send him in and ask him what this all means, right? Call the boy. (ANISYA *exits.*)

AKIM. You look, it's no good, but doing it the right way, God's way, it all somehow, now, it makes you glad, so there's no sin, I mean.

(NIKITA *and* ANYUTKA *enter.)*

NIKITA. You wanted me?

(NIKITA *stands by the table, overly familiarly leaning on it and grinning.)*

AKIM. There's been made, I mean, now, seems like against you, Nikita, a complaint, a complaint, I mean.

NIKITA. Complaint by who?

AKIM. The complaint? By a girl, by a pregnant orphan, I mean, the complaint's by her. By her, and a complaint against you, by Marina, by herself, now.

NIKITA. Makes no sense to me, what you're asking.

AKIM *(portentously)*. Nikita! You can hide from people, but you can't hide from God. You, Nikita, now, think, don't try to lie!

NIKITA. Well, but, there's nothing to say. There was nothing between her and me. (*Spitefully*) The Lord's right there, let me die on the spot. (*Makes the sign of the cross*) I know nothing about nothing. (*Silence*)

MATRYONA (*to her husband*). What'd I tell you, you with your thick old bean, stupid.

PYOTR. Well, what do you think, Uncle Akim? huh?

AKIM (*clucking his tongue; to his son*). Watch yourself, Nikita, the tears of the injured, now, don't just pass by, but every time fall on a man's head. Watch yourself, so it don't come to that.

NIKITA. As for the watching, you yourself watch out. (*Sits*)

ANYUTKA. Got to go tell Mama. (*Runs out*)

NIKITA. All right. *(All exit except* NIKITA. *It gets dark.* NIKITA, *alone, lights a cigarette)* See, they kept pestering, 'come on tell us how you went after the girls'. It'd take a long time to get these stories told. 'Marry her', he says. Yeh and marry 'em all-there'd be a real collection of wives. It's terrible, frightening, they say, to swear to a lie. It's all just stupid. It's nothing, just talk. It's really simple.

AKULINA *(enters in her coat, puts down a rope, takes off her coat and goes to the larder).* You could have at least put the light on.

NIKITA. To look at you? I'd rather see you this way.

AKULINA. Go to hell. (*Exits to the larder. From off*) Nikita! Take a look! Marina herself is coming, sure as I'm living, it's her.

MARINA (*enters*). What're you trying to do to me?

NIKITA. What'm I doing? I'm doing nothing.

MARINA. You want to get rid of me, want to forget.

NIKITA. What's there to remember? I don't need to see you, simple as that. So, go on.

MARINA. Don't need me? You know yourself I never loved no one but you. What'd you stop loving me for? What for?

NIKITA. There's no point in you and me just talking hot air. Go away. You all make no sense.

MARINA. It doesn't hurt me so much that you deceived me, promised to marry me, but you stopped loving me. And it doesn't hurt so much that you stopped loving me as that you swapped me for another-and who for I know! *(NIKITA slaps her.).* What, are you going to beat me? Go ahead, beat me!

NIKITA. Ahh people'll come, it'll look bad, of course. Get out. We're through.

MARINA. So it's the end, means that what was is gone. You tell me to forget! Well, Nikita, remember. I valued my maiden honor more than eyesight. You ruined me for nothing, deceived me. (*cries*) Killed me, you did, but still I don't have it in for you. You find someone better, you'll forget; find someone worse, you'll remember. You'll remember, Nikita. Good-bye, even so. And I loved you, I did. Good-bye for keeps. (*Wants to embrace him and takes his head*)

NIKITA (*tearing himself away*). Don't touch me!

MARINA *(yells)*. You beast! *(In the doorway)* God himself will curse you for what you've done to me! *(Exits crying)*

AKULINA *(comes out of the larder)*. You're a dog, Nikita.

NIKITA. Why?

AKULINA. How she howled! *(Tries to slap him)*

NIKITA. What's that for?

AKULINA. What for? You wronged her- and you lied about it in front of God. You're a dog. *(Exits into the larder)*

NIKITA *(alone, after a silence)*. It's all somehow mixed up. I love the women like sugar, but if you go too far with them- there's trouble!

SCENE 2

The setting is the yard in front of PYOTR'S *peasant cottage, the entranceway-- with the porch in the center; on the right is the gate and edge of the yard. At the edge of the yard is* ANISYA. *Six months have passed since Scene 1.*

ANISYA *(alone).* He's worn me out. Won't let on where the money is, that's the thing. Now I myself don't know where it is. It's still in the house. If only I could find it He's worn me out completely. (MATRYONA *enters with a stick and a bundle* as *if for traveling.)*
MATRYONA. God bless you, sweetie.
ANISYA. *(looks around, drops her work, and claps her hands in joy).* Auntie! God sent just the right guest in time.
MATRYONA. Well?
ANISYA. Oh, I'm all mixed up. It's terrible!
MATRYONA. What do they say, he's alive?
ANISYA. He's neither living nor dying. He can scarce keep body and soul together. He's become just skin and bones. Why just the other day, dearie, he was as good as dead, we put him under the icons. He came to life-got up. Now he's wandering round again.
MATRYONA. He didn't hand the money over to someone?
ANISYA. He's sent for Marfa now, for his own sister. Must be about the money.
MATRYONA. That's clear. He hasn't already slipped it to some-one?
ANISYA. Nobody. I've been watching over him like a hawk.

MATRYONA. Ah, sweetie, he'll hand his bit of money on beyond your reach and you'll weep for ages. You'll get kicked out of the house empty-handed.
ANISYA. Don't talk about it, Auntie. I'm sick at heart, and I don't know where to turn, and I got no one to talk to. I was talking to Nikita. But he's scared, doesn't want to get mixed up in it. Told me just yesterday it's under the floor.
MATRYONA. Well, did you crawl under?
ANISYA. Couldn't-he was there. I've noticed he sometimes carries it with him, sometimes hides it away.
MATRYONA Well, did you treat him to a little of that special tea?
ANISYA. I gave him the powders twice.
MATRYONA. And so he couldn't tell?
ANISYA. I took a sip of the tea myself, just a bit bitter. But he drank them up with his tea and he says: even the tea's turned on me. And I says: everything's bitter for the sick. Oh, I got terrified, Auntie.
MATRYONA. Don't you think about it. The more you think about it the worse it gets. The first thing's to put up the samovar. We'll give him a little tea and then we'll find the money together-we'll get our hands on it, don't worry.
ANISYA. So, I'll go put up the samovar.
MATRYONA. Go, sweetie, do what you got to, so as not to grieve later. (ANISYA *exits,* MATRYONA *beckons to her)* One thing: don't tell Nikita about all this. He's a bit of a fool. God forbid he finds out about the powders, he wouldn't understand this. *(Stops in terror)*
(PYOTR has *appeared on the threshold. Holding to the wall, he comes crawling out onto the porch and calls in a weak voice:)*

PYOTR. Why can't you ever hear me calling? Ah, ah. Anisya, who's here? *(Falls onto the bench)*
ANISYA *(comes from behind the corner)*. What'd you crawl out for? You ought to lie down where you were.
PYOTR. It's terrible! Ah, if only death were quicker! Ah, it's terrible! Ah, this is my death! Ah, I can't stand it no longer. My inside's on fire. It's just like a drill drilling in. They've got rid of me, like a dog-and no one to give me a drink- Ah!
(PYOTR *passes out*)
MATRYONA *(winking)*. Well, dear, remember what you got to do. Go into the house, rummage all around. Hunt like a dog hunts fleas; look through everything, and I'll search on him.
ANISYA *(to* MATRYONA). Right away. I feel a lot braver, seems, with you here. (ANISYA *exits.*)
PYOTR. Hello.
MATRYONA. Oh! Greetings, my dear. You're still ailing, it looks. *(Bows once again)*
PYOTR. I'm dying.
MATRYONA. And now I look at you, Pyotr, it's clear pain don't walk in the forest but falls among men. You've wasted away, you've all wasted away, my dear, I see by looking at you. Ailment, it's clear, don't make a man pretty.
PYOTR. My death has come.
MATRYONA. Ah, so, Pyotr Ignatich, God's will. Your old woman, thank God, is a smart one, and you'll get buried and have prayers said for you all in a fine style. And my boy too will keep busy round the house.
PYOTR. No one to leave it to! Wife's light-headed, busy with foolishness; you see, I know everything-I know- The

girl's a half-wit, and besides, too young. I've set up a house, but there's no one to take care of it. It's a real pity. *(Whimpers)*

ANISYA *(from the entranceway).* Come back in the house, why don't you, I'll help you.

PYOTR. Let me sit here a bit for the last time. It's heavy in there It hurts- Ah, my heart's on fire- If only death-

MATRYONA. In death like in life, it's God's will be done, Pyotr Ignatich. You won't figure out the time of your death, neither.

PYOTR. No. I have a feeling I'll die today, I have a feeling. . . *(Leans back and closes his eyes)*

ANISYA *(enters).* Well, so, you coming or not? A person can't wait all day for you. Pyotr? Hey, Pyotr?

MATRYONA *(steps aside and beckons* ANISYA *over to her with her finger).* Well, so?

ANISYA *(comes down from the porch to* MATRYONA). Nothing there.

MATRYONA. You really looked through everything? Under the floor?

ANISYA. Not there neither. Might be something in the shed. He crawled out there yesterday.

MATRYONA. How's the samovar doing?

ANISYA. Ready to boil.

(NIKITA *comes in from the other side if possible, approaches the gate; does not see* PYOTR.)

NIKITA *(to his mother).* Hello, Ma! Everyone home all right?

MATRYONA. Thank the Lord God, nothing to complain about.

NIKITA. Well, how's the boss?

MATRYONA. He's dead. *(Points to the porch, laughs.)*
NIKITA. So what, let him sit there. What's it to me?
PYOTR *(opens his eyes)*. Nikita, eh, Nikita, come here. (NIKITA *goes toward him,* ANISYA *whispers to* MATRYONYA) How come you're back early?
NIKITA. Finished plowing.
PYOTR. Plow the strip other side of the bridge?
NIKITA. That's a lot farther to go.
PYOTR. Lot farther? You'll have to go special. Should of done 'em together. (ANISYA, *without exposing herself, listens in.)*
MATRYONA *(goes up to them)*. Ah, my boy, why don't you try to do what he wants?
PYOTR. So you now-ah !-dig the potatoes, the women'll-ah !-sort 'em.
ANISYA *(to herself)*. Again he wants to send us all away; must be the money's on him right now. Wants to hide it away some place.
PYOTR. And then-ah!-it'll come time to plant 'em, but they'll be rotted. Ah! I can't take it no longer.
MATRYONA *(runs onto the porch, helps* PYOTR *rise.*) You want to go in?
PYOTR. Take me in. *(Cries out in pain, exits.* MATRYONA *supports him.)*
ANISYA. Oh, my poor, aching head! He was hiding something. He's got a plan, it's clear. *(Goes over to* NIKITA) Well, you said the money is under the floor-it's not there. Where's the money?
NIKITA *(angrily)*. And who the hell knows? Go look yourself.

ANISYA. Oh, Nikita! He's called his sister now, wants to give it to her. I'll get thrown off the place! You, too, better start worrying about this. You said he crept out to the shed last night?
NIKITA. Saw him as he was coming away from there, but where he stuck it, who the hell knows.
ANISYA. Oh, my aching head, I'll go look there myself.
(MATRYONA *comes out of the cottage, goes down to* ANISYA *and* NIKITA*)*
MATRYONA. Don't go nowhere; the money was on him. He couldn't hide it from me.

SCENE 3

PYOTR's *cottage. Interior. Nine months have passed since Scene 2.* ANISYA,. ANYUTKA, MITRICH, *the old hired man are there.*

MITRICH *(enters slowly, takes off his coat).* Oh, merciful Father! So the master ain't back?
ANISYA. What?
MITRICH. Nikita ain't come in from town?
ANISYA. No.
MITRICH. Went on a spree, most likely. Oh, Lord! He's got money, so why not have a spree? But how come Akulina went to town?
ANYUTKA. I heard it myself, Ma. 'I'll buy you a little shawl', he says, 'you can pick it out yourself', he says.
ANISYA. Shameless girl! I can't figure out how to get her out of the house; the whole business can't be worked out. He don't feel like it. And her, too. Hasn't finished his sin yet, with his beauty, see, with his own girl.
MITRICH. Sin, sin, sin! And him her stepfather, too.
ANISYA. It's hard for me, neighbor, oh, so hard! How can the earth bring forth such evil things?!
MITRICH. Oh-oh-oh! Mistress, how do you stand it! Took in a beggar, and now he's making a fool of you. There are millions of you women and girls, but just as one has been born, so she dies. She has neither seen or heard anything. A man will learn something; in the inn, or in prison, or in the army, as I have. But what about a woman? She does not know a thing about God,--no, she does not know one day

from another. They creep about like blind pups, and stick their heads into the manure. *(AKIM enters)*

AKIM *(makes the sign of the. cross, kicks off his bast-shoes and takes his things off)*. Peace to this house. You doing well? Hello, Auntie.

ANISYA. Hello, Uncle. Just come over? Come on in, take your things off.

AKIM. I was just thinking, now, I mean, why don't I go, now, to my boy's, I'll go see my boy. And the boy's home? My boy's in, I mean?

ANISYA. No. Over town.

AKIM *(sits down on the bench)*. I've a little business with him, I mean, now, a little business. I was telling him the other day, I was telling him what I need, my little horse gave out, I mean, the little horse. That's why I came, I mean.

ANISYA. Nikita was telling me. When he comes, you two can talk it over. *(Rises, goes to the stove)* Have some supper, and he'll be here. Mitrich, come to supper, hey, Mitrich!. If only his father would appeal to his conscience, but it's shameful to be telling.

AKIM. What?

ANISYA. Nothing, talking to myself. (NIKITA *enters, drunk, with a bag and a bundle under his arm and with packages wrapped in paper; opens* the *door and stands still.)* Well, pay no attention. *(Continues washing the spoons and does not turn her head when the door opens)*

NIKITA. Anisya, hey wife! Who's come?

(ANISYA *looks up and turns away. She is silent.)*

NIKITA. (*threateningly)* Who's here? Or have y'forgotten?

ANISYA. He'll be swaggering now. Come on in.

NIKITA *(still more threateningly)*. Who's come?
ANISYA *(goes to him and takes his hand)*. Well, come. Come on in the house.
NIKITA *(pulls back)*. Right, y'husband. And what's y'husband called, hey? Say it right.
ANISYA. Oh, go to hell-Nikita.
NIKITA. Right! Y'cow-say my patronymic.
ANISYA. Akimych. Well?
NIKITA *(still in the doorway)*. Right. No, now say my last name.
ANISYA *(laughs and pulls his hand)*. Chilikin. You're really loaded!
NIKITA. Right. *(Holds on to the jamb)* No, now you say which leg Chilikin steps into his house with first?
ANISYA. Oh, stop it-you'll freeze us all.
NIKITA. Say it, which leg first? Y'absolutely got to say.
ANISYA *(to herself)*. I'm fed up now. Well, the left. Come on in, my husband.
NIKITA. Right.
ANISYA. Take a look who's here.
NIKITA. M'father? Why, it's m'father. 'Lo there, Pa. *(Bows to him and puts out his hand)* Our complements to you.
AKIM *(not answering)*. It's the vodka, it's the vodka, I mean, what it does. Dirty business!
NIKITA. Vodka! What, did I drink too much? Abs'lutely at fault, drank with a friend, congrat'lations.
ANISYA. Go lie down, hey.
NIKITA. M'wife, say, where'm I standing.
ANISYA. All right, all right, go lie down. (*Exits.*)

NIKITA. I'll still drink up a samovar full with m'father. Put up the samovar. Akulina, come in, hey.
AKULINA *(all dressed up, comes in with packages. To* NIKITA). What did you throw everything round for? Where's my yarn?
NIKITA. Yarn? Yarn's there. Hey, Mitrich! You there? 'Sleep? Go put the horse away.
AKIM *(does not see* AKULINA *and watches his son)*. What's he doing? The old man, I mean, he's dead tired, he was threshing all day, but he was getting loaded. Put away the horse! I'll be! Dirty business.
MITRICH *(climbs off the stove, puts on his leg wrappings)*. Oh, good Lord! Horse's in the yard, hey? Dead tired, I bet. But look at *him,* the hell with him, the way he swilled it up. Brim full. Oh, Lord! Mikola the Sweet! *(Puts on his coat and goes out to the yard)*
NIKITA *(puts on a sober expression)*. Now you, Pa, don't get offended with me. You think I'm drunk. You and me, Pa, can have a little talk right now. 'member everything. 'bout the money you asked. All that can be done. All that's something we can do. Here!
AKIM *(continues to putter with his gear)*. Ah, my lad, now, I mean, a spring road is not a real road-
NIKITA. What y'mean by that? A talk with a drunk ain't a real talk? Now don't you worry.
AKIM *(shakes his head)*. Eh, eh, eh!
NIKITA. The money, here it is. *(Beaches in his pocket, pulls out his wallet, thumbs through the bills, takes out a ten-ruble bill)* Take it for a horse. Take it for a horse, I can't forget m'father. Abs'lutely won't forget him. On account he's m'father. Here, take it. 'S very simple. Glad to do it. *(Goes to* AKIM *and shoves*

the money at him. AKIM *does not take the money.* NIKITA *grabs his hand)* Take it, I tell you, now I'm giving it to you; glad to do it.

AKIM. I can't, I mean, take it and I can't talk with you, I mean. On account you're, now, not yourself, I mean.

NIKITA. Take it. *(Stuffs the money into* AKIM'S *hand)* That's the way I do things! (*Sees* AKULINA) Akulina, show 'em your presents.

AKULINA. What?

NIKITA. Show 'em your presents.

AKULINA. The presents? Why show them?

NIKITA. Get 'em. Show 'em to Anyutka, I tell you. Get the little shawl. Give it here.

ANISYA. (*Enters*) Look at you, showing off.

NIKITA. Take a look at this!

ANISYA. What's there for me to look at? I never get things, hey? Put it away. *(Brushes the shawl onto the floor)*

AKULINA. Why're you throwing things around? Throw your own stuff around. *(Picks it up)*

NIKITA. Anisya! Look here!

ANISYA. Whose money do you have your sprees with and buy presents for your fatty with? With mine!

AKULINA. What do you mean, yours! You wanted to steal it, but didn't get the chance to. Get out, you! *(Tries to get by, pushes)*

ANISYA. What're you pushing for? I'll push you!

AKULINA. Push me? All right, come on. *(Advances toward her)*

NIKITA. Hey, you two, quit it! *(Stands between them)*

AKULINA. Keeps poking her nose in. You better shut up, keep things to yourself. You think people don't know?
ANISYA. What do they know? Say it, say what they know!
AKULINA. Know something 'bout you.
ANISYA. You're a whore, you live with somebody else's husband.
AKULINA. And you poisoned yours.
ANJSYA *(throws herself at* AKULINA). You're lying!
NIKITA *(holds her back).* Anisya! You've forgotten?
ANISYA. What, you threatening me? I ain't scared of you.
NIKITA. Get out! *(Spins* ANISYA *around and pushes her out)*
ANISYA. I'll go to the police.
NIKITA. Out, I tell you! *(Pushes her out)*
ANISYA *(from behind the door).* I'll hang myself!
NIKITA. I bet.
ANYUTKA. Oh-oh! Mama dearest, my Mama. *(Cries)*
AKULINA *(gathers the packages, puts them away).* Ugh, the foul bitch, what a stink she made!
NIKITA. I chased her out, what more d'y'want?
AKULINA. She got my new shawl dirty. A real bitch. If she hadn't gone, I would of scratched her eyes out.
NIKITA. Ah, you can't make a woman shut up with nothing. I'm the boss. I do what I want. Stopped loving her, started loving you. I love who I want. That's my right.
AKIM *(slides off and puts on his fur coat; goes over to the table, puts the bill on it).* Here's your money. Put it away.
NIKITA *(does not see the bill).* Where you going?
AKIM. I'm going, going, now, for the Lord's sake, forgive me. *(Takes his hat)*

NIKITA. What the hell's this? Where y'going to do anything at night now?
AKIM. I can't, I mean, I can't, now, stay in your house, can't stay, forgive me.
NIKITA. What're you leaving the tea for?
AKIM *(puts on his coat)*. I'm leaving, 'cause, I mean, things're wrong in your place, I mean, now, wrong, Nikita, wrong, in your house. I mean, you're living sin, Nikita, sin. I told you, now, 'bout the orphan girl, Marina, I mean. One sin, I mean, leads to another, pulls it on after itself, and you, Nikita, you've got mired in sin. Got mired, got bogged down, I mean. *(Exits)*
NIKITA. (*drinks from a flask*)You're breaking up the party.

SCENE 4

Autumn. Evening. The moon is shining. The yard outside the cottage.

A NEIGHBOR. How come Akulina ain't come out?
NEIGHBOR. How come she ain't come out? The matchmakers came to look the bride over, but she, my dear, is lying in the summerhouse and don't so much as poke her nose out, poor thing.
A NEIGHBOR. How come?
NEIGHBOR. 'Tween you and me, they say she's got Cramps.
A NEIGHBOR. Not really!?
NEIGHBOR. Really. *(Whispers in her ear)*
A NEIGHBOR. So? That's real bad. And 'course the matchmakers'll find out.
NEIGHBOR. How'll they ever find out? They're all drunk. Besides, they're mostly after the dowry. It's easy enough, they're giving the girl with two fur coats, my dear, six housecoats, a French shawl, also a lot of linen and, they were saying, a couple of hundred rubles.
A NEIGHBOR. Well, and even with that money you can't be happy. It's a terrible shame.
NEIGHBOR. Shhh-the matchmaker don't know nothing. *(They stop talking and enter the doorway. The MATCHMAKER comes out of the doorway alone, hiccoughing.)*
MATCHMAKER. I'm all sweaty. Awful hot. Got to cool off a bit. *(Stands, takes a big breath)* God knows what's going on...something ain't right, don't make me feel good...
MATRYONA *(comes out from the same doorway)*. And I'm

looking all over: where's the matchmaker, where's the matchmaker? And here you are, my dear- And so, my dear, thank the Lord, it all came out right honorably.

MATCHMAKER. Seems not bad, the whole business, but we got to keep our eyes open about the money.

MATRYONA. Don't talk about the money. Whatever it was her family give her - it all goes with her. Nowadays it's something, too.

MATCHMAKER. It's for our own child. You want everything good as you can.

MATRYONA. And I'm telling you the truth, Matchmaker: if it wasn't for me, you would of never found her in your life.

MATCHMAKER. Seems not bad, the whole business. My old woman and me's been noticing something about the girl, though. How come she ain't come out? We're thinking, maybe she's ailing?

MATRYONA. Oh, oh-she's ailing!? 'Deed there's none in the district like her. The girl's like iron-can't hurt her.

MATCHMAKER. Welllll......., all right. The thing's settled.

MATRYONA. Right, right, you've agreed, and no backing out.

MATCHMAKER'S WIFE. (*comes out from inside*) It's time we were going, Ivan, come on.

MATCHMAKER. Right away. *(they exit.)*

NIKITA *(enters; is silent; sits down).* Ah, what a mess! Akulina is making such a racket in the barn.

ANISYA. What're you sitting here for? No time to be sitting around. Got to carry it away right now.

NIKITA. What'll we do?

ANISYA. I told you what. So go do it.
NIKITA. Yeh, you'd put it in the foundling home, wouldn't you?
ANISYA. Go and take it yourself, if you want to. You're a dainty one for dirty tricks, I see, but pretty weak at getting out of 'em.
NIKITA. What'll I do?
ANISYA. I tell you, go in the cellar and dig a hole.
NIKITA. But you can figure out something else.
ANISYA *(mocking him)*. Something else! You ought to of been thinking about this 9 months earlier. Go where you're told.
NIKITA. Ah, what a mess, what a mess! (ANYUTKA *enters.)*
ANYUTKA. Mama! Gramma's calling. I bet Sis's got a baby, sure as I'm living, it cried out.
ANISYA. What're you making up now? Some kittens are whining there, that's all. Get into the house and go to bed. Or I'll give you one-
ANYUTKA. Mama, Mama, it's the truth, so help me God--
ANISYA *(threatens her)*. I'll give you one! And not a peep from you! (ANYUTKA *runs out. To* NIKITA) Go on, do what you're told. Or watch out! *(Exits)*
NIKITA *(alone, is long silent)*. Ah, what a mess! Oh, these women! It's no good! You, she says, ought to of been thinking earlier. When earlier to think of it? When to think 'bout it at all? Well, so what? You think I'm a monk? Wasn't all my doing. Akulina started hanging round. What's the difference to me? If it wasn't me, it would of been somebody else. And now it's this far! And again it wasn't any

of my doing. Oh, what a mess! *(Sits reflectively)* These women got guts-what they figured out. But I ain't going to do that.
MATRYONA *(comes out in a hurry with a lantern and a spade).* What're you sitting here for, like a chicken on an egg? What'd your old woman tell you to do? Get it ready. We'll fix it up so there won't be the littlest scent. Just do what I tell you. Here's the spade, now, so crawl down there and fix it up. I'll hold the light.
NIKITA. Fix up what?
MATRYONA *(in a whisper).* Dig a little hole. And then we'll bring it out. Go on, go on.
NIKITA. But, is it dead?
MATRYONA. Sure, it's dead. Just you got to move quickly. 'cause people ain't turned in yet. They'll hear, they got to know everything, the bastards. Crawl into the cellar. Dig a little hole in the corner there, the earth's soft, and then you can smooth it over again. Go on. Go on!
NIKITA. You're getting me all mixed up in it. The hell with you all. Do it yourselves best you can.
ANISYA *(from the doorway).* Well, did he get it dug, hey?
MATRYONA. Why'd you leave her? What'd you do with it?
ANISYA. Covered it up with a piece of burlap. Nobody'll hear it. Did he get it dug?
MATRYONA. He won't!
ANISYA *(jumping out, in a rage).* He won't! I'll go right to the police, tell 'em everything. Go down together. I'll tell everything right this minute.
NIKITA *(dumb-struck).* What'll you tell 'em?
ANISYA. What? Everything! Who took the money? You! (NIKITA is *silent)* And who gave the poison? I did! But you

knew! I was in agreement with you! Go on, I tell you, or I'll do what I said!- Take the spade, take it! Go on!
NIKITA. Hold on, now; what do you insist for? *(Takes the spade, but hesitates)* No, I won't do it--won't go down.
ANISYA. Won't go? *(Begins to shout)* Hey, everybody!
MATRYONA *(covers her mouth).* What're you doing? You crazy? He'll go-- Go on, my boy, go on, my dear. (NIKITA *goes to the cellar)* That's the way it is, sweetie: you knew how to splurge, now you got to know how to cover your tracks. (*to* ANISYA) Don't you get mad, dear; do things quietly and bit by bit; that's the best way. Go to the girl now. He'll do it. (NIKITA *crawls into the cellar*) He's digging. Go get it.
ANISYA. Stay with him. Or the bastard'll run away. (*Exits. Sounds of digging.* AKULINA *screams from offstage.* ANISYA *reenters with the baby wrapped in rags.*) Took it from her by force-wouldn't let go. (*Goes up to and gives it to* NIKITA)
NIKITA *(takes it).* It's alive! Mother of God, it's moving! it's alive! What'll I do with it?
ANISYA *(grabs the baby out of his arms and throws it into the cellar).* Hurry up and smother it and it won't be alive. *(Pushes* NIKITA *down)* It's your business, you finish it.
ANISYA *(looking into the cellar).* He's covered it up with a board, and sat down on it. Must of finished.
NIKITA. (*Reappears.*) What've they done? What've they done to me? It whined so-- How it crunched under me. And it's alive, still, really, it's alive! *(Stops talking and listens)* It's whining- Listen, it's whining. (*listens by the cellar entrance. Walks on. Stops.)* And how the little bones crunched under me. Crr-crr- *(Again listens)* Again it's whining, really, it's whining, oh, Mama! *(Goes over to her)*

MATRYONA. Go on in, dear, and have a drink. A day or two'll pass, and you won't think about it no more. We'll marry the girl off and we won't think about it no more. Go have a drink now.
ANISYA. Well, had your fun? You lived in grand style, now you wait, you'll find out yourself what it's like. You'll come down a peg.
NIKITA. Mother, Mama! *(listens).* It's alive. Don't you hear it? it's alive! Listen-it's whining. There distinctly-
MATRYONA. And how could it be whining? You know you flattened it out like a pancake. You smashed its whole little head.
NIKITA. What?! *(covers his ears)* It's still whining! I've ruined my own life! Ruined it! What've they done to me?! Where can I go?! *(Sits down on the steps, drinks from a flask)*

SCENE 5

The Yard the next morning. It is the day of the wedding. Nikita lays face down in the mud. MARINA enters.

MARINA *(alone; is lost in thought)* Well, well. The stepfather of the bride! Or are you the defeated suitor? One can never tell these things with you, Nikita. The fox changes his coat with the seasons.
NIKITA *(rolls over, catches sight of* MARINA, *recognizes her).* Marina! Dear friend, Marinushka! Why're you here?
MARINA. The wedding.
NIKITA. Then you've come to laugh at me.
MARINA. What should I laugh at you for? I came with my husband.
NIKITA. Eh, Marinushka! *(Tries to embrace her)*
MARINA *(breaks away angrily).* Oh, Nikita, you stop doing this. What's past is past. I came with my husband. He'll be along any minute. Why are you out here instead of getting ready?
NIKITA *(sits down).* Why am I out here? Eh, if you only knew, if you only knew! I'm sad, Marina, I'm so sad my eyes couldn't look no more
MARINA *(goes over closer to him).* What's wrong?
NIKITA. Something I can't eat up by eating, drink up by drinking, sleep off by sleeping. I feel sick, so sick! And I feel sickest of all, Marina, being alone and having nobody to share my grief with.
MARINA. But what's wrong?

NIKITA. Ah, what's made me sick of my whole life. I'm sick of myself. Eh, Marina, you didn't know how to hold on to me, and you ruined me and yourself, too! You think this is life?

MARINA *(stands by the barn, cries and tries to contain herself)*. I ain't complaining about my own life, Nikita. My old man's quiet and considerate to me. What've I got to be bitter about? It's clear, that's the way God wanted it. But what's wrong with your life? You got money-

NIKITA. My life! Only I don't want to break up the wedding. I'd take a rope, and I'd toss it right over a beam in the barn there. And I'd fix up a real good loop, and I'd climb up on the beam, and put my head right in. That's what my life's like!

MARINA. You mean it? God help you!

NIKITA. You think I'm joking? Think I'm drunk? I ain't drunk. Today I ain't a bit tight. But grief, grief's eaten me up completely. Eaten me up so, that nothing seems good to me! What can I do with my feelings? Where can I go now?

MARINA. What can you do? You got your own wife, don't make eyes at others, but take care of your own. You loved Anisya, so go on loving her.

NIKITA. Ah, this Anisya's like bitter wormwood to me, only she's wrapped herself round my legs, like witchgrass. Here's your husband coming, calling you. Go now.

MARINA. And what'll you do?

NIKITA. Me? I'll lie here a bit. Where'll I go now? Ah! Open wide, sweet mother earth! *(Lies down in the mud.*

MARINA *moves toward Nikita, but stops, turns and goes off stage)*

ANYUTKA *(enters; sees* NIKITA *and runs over to him).* Pa, oh, Pa! Everyone's here for the wedding!!
NIKITA *(to himself).* Where'll I go now?
ANYUTKA. What? What'd you say?
NIKITA. Didn't say nothing. What're you after me for?
ANYUTKA. Pa! Let's go! (NIKITA *is silent.* ANYUTKA *pulls him by the hand)* Pa, come and bless 'em! Honest and true, everybody's here.
NIKITA *(pulls his hand away).* Leave me alone!
ANYUTKA. What now!
NIKITA *(threatens her).* Get out of here, I tell you. Or I'll give it to you.
ANYUTKA. Then I'll get Mama. *(Runs off)*
NIKITA *(alone; gets up).* Now how'll I go? How'll I take the icon? How'll I look her in the eye? *(Lies down again)* Oh, if only there was a hole in the earth, I'd go in. People wouldn't see me, and I wouldn't see no one. *(Again gets up)* I won't go - Let 'em perish! Won't go. *(picks up a rope; makes a loop in it, throws it around his neck)* Do it like this.
(MATRYONA *enters.* NIKITA *sees his mother, takes the rope off his head and lies down again on the straw.)*
MATRYONA *(comes up in a hurry).* Nikita! Nikita, what's wrong with you, you drunk? Come on, Nikitushka, come on, come on, sweetie. The people're arriving.
NIKITA. Ah, what've you all done to me? I ain't a man no more.
MATRYONA. What're you talking about? Come on, dear, do the blessing and all the honors and have it over with. Everybody's coming, see?

(The yard fills with people. They are singing "V Tyomnom Lese". AKULINA *and the groom are in the front.. Among the guests are* MARINA, *her husband, and the policeman.* ANISYA *carries vodka. The singing dies down.)*
BEST MAN. Well, Good Lord! Here's the stepfather's going to give his blessing. But hey, don't get dressed up on our account!!
ANISYA. Don't worry, have a little bit more to drink.
(The women sing. Men point and talk in derisive tones. There is general revelry and hubbub. AKIM *enters and pulls NIKITA to his feet.)*
NIKITA *(to the women).* That's enough, be quiet. *(Looks around at everyone in the yard)* Look at me. Brothers and Sisters, you're all here, and I'm here! Here I am as I am! *(Falls on his knees)*
ANISYA. Nikita, what's wrong with you? Oh, my aching head I --
MATCHMAKER. I never!
MATRYONA. And I'm telling you: he's had too much of the French wine, too much. Pull yourself together, what's wrong with you? *(Tries to pick him up; he pays no attention to anyone, stares straight in front of himself)*
NIKI TA. Brothers and Sisters! I'm guilty, and I'm going to confess.
MATRYONA *(plucks his shoulder).* What's wrong with you, you crazy? Got to take him away.
NIKITA *(pushes her away with his shoulder).* Leave me alone! But you, Pa, you listen. First thing: Marina, look here. *(Bends down to her feet and gets up)* I am guilty toward you, promised to

marry you, seduced you. I deceived you, left you, forgive me for the Lord's sake! *(Again bows down to her feet)*

ANISYA. What're you babbling like this for? It's got nothing to do with nothing at all. Nobody's asking you for it.

MATRYONA. Oh-oh, something unnatural's come over him. What're you muttering such stupid stuff for? *(Pulls him)*

NIKITA *(shakes his head)*. Don't touch me! Forgive, Marina, the sin I did to you. Forgive for the Lord's sake.

(MARINA *covers her face with her hands and is silent.)*

ANISYA. Get up, I tell you. Better think what you're doing. It's shameful!

NIKITA *(pushes his wife away, turns toward* AKULINA). Akulina, what I've to say now is for you. You listen, Brothers and Sisters! I am damned! Akulina! I'm guilty toward You. Your father didn't die his own death. He was poisoned with poison. *(Crowd reacts.)*

ANISYA *(screams)*. MY aching head! What's he doing ?

MATRYONA. Man's out of his mind. Take him away.

(People draw closer, want to seize him.)

AKIM *(pushes them away with his hands)*. Stop! You, fellows, stop, now.

NIKITA. Akulina, I gave him poison. Forgive me for the Lord's sake.

AKULINA.. He's lying! I know who--

MATCHMAKER. What're you doing? You sit down.

AKIM. Oh, God! it's a sin, it's a sin.

POLICEMAN. Grab him! And get the magistrate and the witnesses. Got to draw up a statement. You, there, get up, come here.

AKIM *(toward the policeman).* Now you, I mean, you just wait. Let him have his say, now.

POLICEMAN *(toward* AKIM). Look out, old man, don't butt in. I'm required to draw up a statement.

AKIM. Likes of you, now. Just wait, I tell you. Here God's work's being done A man's confessing, I mean.

POLICEMAN. Call the magistrate!

AKIM. Let God's work be done, I mean, then, you can do yours.

NIKITA. My sin toward you, Akulina, is still greater: I seduced you, forgive me for the Lord's sake! *(Bows down to her feet)*

AKULINA . Let me go, I won't get married. He told me to, but now I won't.

POLICEMAN. Repeat what you said.

NIKITA. Just wait, Mr. Policeman, let me say it all.

AKIM *(in ecstasy).* Speak, my child, say everything, it'll be easier. Confess to God, don't fear the others. God, now-God! Here He is!

NIKITA. I poisoned the father, I, like a dog, destroyed the daughter, too. I had the power over her, destroyed her baby, too.

AKULINA. It's true, it's true.

NIKITA. I smothered her baby with a board down in the cellar. Sat on it -smothered it- and the little bones in it crunched. *(Cries)* And I dug it a hole in the ground. I did it, did it myself alone!

AKULINA. He's lying. I told him to.

NIKITA. Don't you protect me. I ain't scared of nobody now. Forgive me, Brothers and Sisters! *(Bows down to the ground) (Silence.)*
POLICEMAN. Tie him up; your wedding, of course, is put off. *(People draw up with their belts.)*
NIKITA. Wait, you'll have time. *(Bows down to his father's feet)* Father, my father, you too forgive me, cursed man that I am! You told me from the first, when I set out on this wicked wandering, you told me: "If one claw gets caught, the whole bird's lost," but, like a dog, I didn't listen to what you said, and it came like you said it would. Forgive me for the Lord's sake.
AKIM *(in ecstasy)*. God'll forgive, my dear child. *(Embraces him)* Didn't spare yourself, he'll spare you. God, now, God, now! Here He is!
MAGISTRATE *(enters)*. Lots of witnesses here.
POLICEMAN. We'll make the examination right away. *(They tie and bind* NIKITA.)
NIKITA *(tied up)*. There's nothing to ask. I did it all myself, alone. It was my design and my own deed. Take me where you want to. I won't say nothing more.

[*End of play*]

www.ingramcontent.com/pod-product-compliance
Ingram Content Group UK Ltd.
Pitfield, Milton Keynes, MK11 3LW, UK
UKHW020229250726
13967UKWH00001B/265

9 780557 513727